# Judith of Bethulia

## A BURLESQUE BASED ON ANCIENT THEMES

## by Charles Busch

A SAMUEL FRENCH ACTING EDITION

SAMUEL FRENCH
FOUNDED 1830

SAMUELFRENCH.COM

**ISBN 978-0-573-70094-1**     Printed in U.S.A.     #20490

## MUSIC USE NOTE

Licensees are solely responsible for obtaining formal written permission from copyright owners to use copyrighted music in the performance of this play and are strongly cautioned to do so. If no such permission is obtained by the licensee, then the licensee must use only original music that the licensee owns and controls. Licensees are solely responsible and liable for all music clearances and shall indemnify the copyright owners of the play and their licensing agent, Samuel French, Inc., against any costs, expenses, losses and liabilities arising from the use of music by licensees.

## IMPORTANT BILLING AND CREDIT
## REQUIREMENTS

All producers of *JUDITH OF BETHULIA* must give credit to the Author of the Play in all programs distributed in connection with performances of the Play, and in all instances in which the title of the Play appears for the purposes of advertising, publicizing or otherwise exploiting the Play and/or a production. The name of the Author *must* appear on a separate line on which no other name appears, immediately following the title and *must* appear in size of type not less than fifty percent of the size of the title type.

In addition the following credit *must* be given in all programs and publicity information distributed in association with this piece:

**Judith of Bethulia was developed at Theatre For the New City
(Crystal Field, Executive Artistic Director) in New York City in April 2012**

*JUDITH OF BETHULIA* was first produced by Theater for the New City in their Cino Theatre in New York City on March 30, 2012. The performance was directed by Carl Andress, with lighting by Kirk Bookman, costumes by Jessica Jahn, sets by Brian Whitehill, wigs and headdresses by Katherine Carr and sound by Jill BC Duboff. The production Stage Manager was Trisha Henson. The cast was as follows:

| | |
|---|---|
| **JUDITH** | Charles Busch |
| **ARGA** | Mary Testa |
| **HOLOFERNES** | John Wojda |
| **NATHAN, LEPER, CITIZEN #1** | Jennifer Van Dyck |
| **URDAMANI, STARVING MAN** | Christopher Borg |
| **NAOMI** | Jennifer Cody |
| **SIMON, LEPER, CITIZEN #2** | Billy Wheelan |
| **OZIAS, MORDECHAI** | Kendal Sparks |
| **THOR, CAPTAIN** | Larry Bullock |
| **CONAN, CAPTAIN #2** | Dave August |

# CHARACTERS

(Please Note: This play can be double cast, as well as cross-gender cast.)

JUDITH

ARGA

HOLOFERNES

NATHAN

LEPER

CITIZEN #1

URDAMANI

STARVING MAN

NAOMI

SIMON

LEPER

CITIZEN #2

OZIAS

MORDECHAI

THOR

CONAN

CAPTAIN

CAPTAIN #2

# PROLOGUE

(**NATHAN**, *an impassioned handsome youth addresses the audience.*)

**NATHAN.** I have only the briefest of time. With our world in upheaval, allow me to present myself simply and without flourish. I am Nathan; a poet who circumstance has forged into a soldier. I am but one of a legion of beardless youths. We are boys willing to sacrifice the springtime of our lives to fight tyranny. This is the time for action, for ejaculations of "JUSTICE!" I shall now return you to those months not long ago, when the Assyrians first demanded our walled city of Bethulia be a gateway to their conquest of all of Judea. To that end, Bethulia was doomed for destruction. Our Patriarchs made a futile attempt to reason with the King of Assyria's Chief General, Holofernes, but coming to terms with that tyrant meant only one thing; capitulation. And capitulation meant submission. And submission meant surrender. And surrender meant slaughter. And slaughter meant obliteration. And obliteration meant this be bad. However, on the fair morn where my tale unfolds, the flowers were buzzin' with the hum of bees. The sky was a bright canary yellow. The larks were learning to pray. And the good citizens of Bethulia still hoped for a peaceful resolution to the King of Assyria's mad thirst for power. Unbeknownst to any, General Holofernes, himself a Prince of Judea, accompanied by his faithful eunuch, slipped into Bethulia in disguise. Their mere presence poisoned the air of the market place.

## SCENE ONE

*(The market place. An elderly blind man,* **MORDECHAI**, *enters, carrying a basket of fruit.* **HOLOFERNES** *and his eunuch,* **URDAMANI**, *enter from the other side.)*

**MORDECHAI.** Olives! Figs! Oranges! Only two weeks old! Olives! Figs! Oranges! Get 'em while you're still alive!

**URDAMANI.** General, I do love a masquerade. Not a soul would ever recognize us.

**HOLOFERNES.** If they do, their entrails shall be strewn throughout this market place.

**URDAMANI.** And if I might add, your Excellency, those rags look splendid on you. However voluminous, one can still discern the lines of your superb physique.

**HOLOFERNES.** It was not my intention to expose my *pulchritude.* I am forced by circumstance to be nude under these robes, for during the night some thief stole my thong.

*(***URDAMANI*** averts his guilty face.)*

But was it quite necessary for *you* to masquerade in the garb of a woman?

**URDAMANI.** 'Twas was all I could find in the thrift shop, General. Not a one of these Jews have paid me any heed.

**HOLOFERNES.** They are too busy worshipping their invisible God and making mockery of their Sovereign. Eunuch, we must be devoid of eccentricity. Our aim is to observe the common folk with the utmost discretion and take note of their every weakness.

**URDAMANI.** I shall do my best, my Lord, to perfect my female impersonation to blend in with the crowd.

**HOLOFERNES.** If that is indeed your intention, Urdamani, then you needn't sashay your hips quite so much. A real woman moves with the simplicity of a desert breeze.

URDAMANI. Your Highness, there is much I can learn from you of being a man and a woman.

HOLOFERNES. Urdamani., the mysteries of a woman are profound. The sight of her alabaster skin, the taste of her lips, the sounds of her moaning in desire and above all, Urdamani, above all her scent. The pungent, sweet, luxuriant smell of a woman's most intimate depths.

(URDAMANI *begins to gag.*)

URDAMANI. Forgive me, your Excellency.

(ARGA, *a servant woman, enters carrying a large full satchel. She sees* MORDECHAI.)

MORDECHAI. Fruit! Fresh fruit for sale!

ARGA. Mordechai, are you still trying to palm off those rotten navel oranges?

MORDECHAI. Arga, my good and loyal friend.

ARGA. Mordechai, you're looking pinched and sickish. I don't like it. Here, take a few of these grapefruits. *(She takes two out of her satchel.)*

MORDECHAI. It is not right, Arga. You purchased these for your mistress, Judith.

ARGA. *(contemptuously) She'll* never know. Take three. Eat one. Resell two.

MORDECHAI. A thousand blessings on you, dear Arga.

(HOLOFERNES *and* URDAMANI *approach her.*)

HOLOFERNES. Good woman, we are travelers new to Bethulia. And regretfully ignorant of its history and customs.

ARGA. Bethulia would be a charming vacation spot if we weren't facing ANNIHILATION.

HOLOFERNES. What of the mood of the people? Do they feel defeated?

ARGA. *(suspiciously)* Defeated? Who are you and where are you from? There are spies in every corner.

**HOLOFERNES**. I am no spy. Merely a vagabond artisan from Damascus. And this is… this is….

**URDAMANI**. *(with soft feminine allure)* I am his wife.

**ARGA**. *(with a squint)* Are you a Jew? You don't look Jewish.

**URDAMANI**. *(overplaying the Jewish inflection)* Am I ever? Lox and bagels. Oy yoy yoy.

**HOLOFERNES**. *(diverting attention from **URDAMANI**)* The fighting is perilously close. Surely there are other markets nearer to your home.

**ARGA**. Indeed they are. But this market sells a particular kind of grapefruit that my mistress dotes on. I risk my personal safety to accommodate her every whim.

**HOLOFERNES**. Who is your mistress?

**ARGA**. Judith, widow of the land owner, Manasses.

**HOLOFERNES**. Ah, the widow of Manasses. Her great beauty is the stuff of legend.

**ARGA**. You should see her in the morning.

**HOLOFERNES**. It is said she hails from the far off banks of the River Jordan.

**ARGA**. Yeah. The *left* bank.

**URDAMANI**. You don't care much for your mistress, do you?

**ARGA**. You're something of a gossip. Aren't you? I don't gossip. I'm a truth teller. It's an affliction. My mistress is an awful creature. I don't care who hears me. After a whirlwind courtship, she married my master, a much older man, a pillar of the community. Did I say an extremely wealthy man? He died suddenly and a brand new will was revealed, leaving everything to his widow.

**URDAMANI**. Are you suggesting that your mistress murdered her husband?

**ARGA**. Control yourself, dear. I'm not suggesting anything of the kind. But let me just say that old Manasses was under the thrall of that woman. She emits a kind of musk that drives men to a frenzy.

**HOLOFERNES**. *(titillated)* A musk, you say? How long have you been a part of your mistress's household?

**ARGA**. *(portentously)* I came to the House of Manasses with the first wife – Ruchel.

*(That last statement is accompanied by a dramatic music cue. **NAOMI**, a young prostitute, runs on. We hear shouts from the angry mob chasing her.)*

VOICES. Stone the whore! Kill her!

**ARGA**. What's going on?

*(**NAOMI** grabs on to **ARGA** in terror and tries to hide behind her.)*

**NAOMI**. Save me! Please! I beg of you!

**ARGA**. Who is chasing you, girl?

**NAOMI**. A Patriarch has accused me of trading my body for coins. It was he who made crude advances. Help me get away. If I'm caught, I shall be stoned to death.

**ARGA**. What have they done with your clothes?

**NAOMI**. Forgive my fashion faux pas. A series of personal tragedies have forced me into a life of sin.

**ARGA**. *(seemingly sympathetic)* My child, are you then a prostitute?

**NAOMI**. Only on Tuesdays.

**ARGA**. *(mulling it over)* Only on Tuesdays. *(shouting)* Here she is! Here is the fallen woman!!

*(**NAOMI** tries to break away from **ARGA**'s grip)*

**NAOMI**. What are you doing?

**ARGA**. Bringing a whore to justice! *(to the offstage mob)* Boys, we've got plenty of rocks over here!!

**NAOMI**. Let me go! Let go of me!

*(**NAOMI** breaks free of **ARGA** and runs off.)*

**ARGA**. She went that a way!

**HOLOFERNES**. You are a woman of strong conviction.

**ARGA**. We must get the riff-raff off the streets. Why won't people listen to me? Stoning acts as a deterrent! Speaking of riff raff, here comes my mistress.

**HOLOFERNES**. A woman of her class traversing the open marketplace?

**URDAMANI**. Scandalous!

**ARGA**. She has an insatiable appetite for acquiring baubles, trinkets and fabrics. She's a hoarder.

(**JUDITH** *is carried in on her litter by two large, muscular bearers,* **THOR** *and* **CONAN**. *Bedecked and bejeweled,* **JUDITH** *has both the exotic grandeur of Sarah Bernhardt and the jaunty, good natured swagger of Mae West. Well, maybe a bit more Mae West. Well, maybe a lot more Mae West.*)

**JUDITH**. Boys, halt.

**THOR**. Yes, mistress?

**JUDITH**. Is that peddler selling jewelry?

**THOR**. Yes, mistress. Gems of every kind. Would you care to dismount?

**JUDITH**. Tempting though it is, I suppose I do have my fair share of turquoise, opals and marcasites. Where are the woolens?

**ARGA**. *(to* **HOLOFERNES***)* As you see, my mistress is oblivious to my very presence.

**HOLOFERNES**. So that is the widow of Manasses. She is exquisite.

**URDAMANI**. *(jealous) She* has her bad angles.

**JUDITH**. Oh, hello, Arga. I couldn't see you among all those dried fruits.

**ARGA**. *(coldly)* Mistress, you have no need to acknowledge me. I am merely a cog in your household, as insignificant as a wooden spoon.

**JUDITH**. Boys, bring me down to her level.

(**CONAN** *and* **THOR** *lower the litter.* **JUDITH** *rises.*)

**JUDITH**. You can park the litter.

(*The boys move the litter to the side of the stage.* **JUDITH** *turns to* **ARGA**.)

Arga, I respect your devotion to your late mistress, but there is no reason on earth why we shouldn't get along.

**ARGA**. I have no quarrel with you, Widow.

**JUDITH**. But you don't like me. Have I treated you badly? I don't think so. Have I ever beat you? Not a finger have I ever raised. Have I been miserly with your wages? It's a known fact that you're the highest paid servant in all of Judea and with a RETIREMENT PLAN! WHY ARE YOU NOT CONTENT?

**ARGA**. We are not on this earth to seek contentment but to glean from suffering.

**JUDITH**. I don't think that philosophy is doing much for you.

*(Cries are heard of "Lepers! Lepers!" The* **LEPERS** *cower in the corner.)*

**JUDITH**. What did they say?

**MORDECHAI**. Lepers! Lepers!

**ARGA**. They're lepers who have ventured from the Valley of Death. They shall bring death to us all!

**MORDECHAI**. Lepers! Lepers!

**JUDITH**. We heard you. They're lepers.

**HOLOFERNES**. The Valley and all of its inhabitants should be burned.

**JUDITH**. *(calling out to the lepers)* Come closer. Yes, you there. Cowering by the chick peas.

**CONAN**. Do not let them near you, Mistress.

**JUDITH**. I have no fear.

*(The frightened* **LEPERS** *approach the litter.)*

**ARGA**. She's mad.

**MORDECHAI**. Lepers! Lepers!

**JUDITH**. Have you bread to eat and water to drink?

**LEPER #1**. We have only what is left for us at the foot of the Valley of Death. Often that small bit of sustenance is stolen from us by scavengers.

(**JUDITH** *presents the* **LEPER** *with her purse full of coins.*)

**JUDITH.** Here. Take these silver talents and may the good Lord be with you.

(**JUDITH** *gently touches the* **LEPER**'s *hand. Inspirational music is heard.*)

**ARGA.** She touched a leper! Did you see that? She touched a leper!

**MORDECHAI.** Lepers! Lepers!

**LEPER #2.** You touched my hand. Bless you, great lady, bless you.

(**LEPER #2** *rubs his runny nose beneath his layers of rags.*)

**JUDITH.** Don't rub your nose, dear. It's hanging by a thread. You need some color. Here, take this scarf.

(*She gives* **LEPER #2** *a scarf that's among her things on the litter.*)

**LEPER #2.** I cannot comprehend such kindness. *(Drapes the scarf around his wrist.)*

**JUDITH.** That's nice. Breaks things up. *(to* **LEPER #1***)* And you, dear. Take this bangle. Yeah. Put it on.

(*She removes a bracelet and gives it to the* **LEPER**, *who puts it on.*)

**LEPER** #1. It glitters like the stars above.

**JUDITH.** Looks cute on you.

**LEPER** #1. I love it.

**JUDITH.** This has been fun but you better head back to the Valley, before the crowd turns ugly.

**LEPERS.** Blessings! Blessings! Blessings!

**JUDITH.** Good luck to you.

(*The* **LEPERS** *run off.* **HOLOFERNES** *approaches her.*)

**HOLOFERNES.** You have courage, Madame, to consort with these revolting living corpses.

**JUDITH**. Only cruelty disgusts me. I live by the teachings of the Torah.

**HOLOFERNES**. I would never take you for a Jewess. Your features are not of a coarse Hebraic cast.

**JUDITH**. I see nothing superior in a finely chiseled nose.

(**HOLOFERNES** *begins sniffing her skin*)

What are you sniffing at? You got a sinus?

**HOLOFERNES**. There is something about you. A powerful and intriguing scent.

**JUDITH**. Perhaps it is my perfume, culled from my very own lavender fields.

**HOLOFERNES**. It's more than a perfume. It is your feminine essence.

**JUDITH**. I'm finding the turn of this discourse not only vulgar and inappropriate but downright disgusting.

**URDAMANI**. *(with hauteur)* My husband is a general - I mean a gentleman of the highest refinement. If you mistake his words for vulgar discourse, it is you, Madame, who is rolling in the mire.

**JUDITH**. Were you part of this conversation?

**HOLOFERNES**. Charming lady, it is most regretful that my sensual observations have caused you distress. My "wife" and I must be on our travels. Good day to you.

(**HOLOFERNES** *and* **URDAMANI** *exit just as* **NAOMI** *is chased on once more. The offstage mob is heard again. The "***LEPERS***" could return again, now garbed as irate* **CITIZENS**.*)*

CITIZENS. Stone the whore! Kill her!

**NAOMI**. Shelter! Protection! Please! The angry mob will kill me!

**ARGA**. Let he who hath no sin, cast the first stone. That's me! *(She picks a rock off the ground.)* If I'm careful, I can get her right between the eyes.

**JUDITH**. Arga! Leave her be! I should like to speak to the girl.

**ARGA.** She's nothing but a common tramp.

CITIZEN #1. The whore!

**JUDITH.** Why you're scarcely more than a child.

CITIZEN #2. She's a whore!

**JUDITH.** Talk to me, my girl.

**MORDECHAI.** Even blind I can tell she's a whore!

**JUDITH.** Speak, pray.

**NAOMI.** I am all of fifteen. But I feel forty-five. My flesh bears the stain of every man who has defiled me. I come from simple farm stock. My father attempted to marry me off to a neighbor, as a way of protecting the boundaries of his land. On the eve of my wedding, I was ravaged by three men, friends of my betrothed. I was blamed for luring them and cast off into the night. I found my way to a port town, full of shops and fine ethnic dining. But try as I may, there were no employment opportunities that didn't involve at least cunnilingus. God, I hate men! Damn them! Every father's son of them! DAMN THEM ALL!!!

**JUDITH.** You've had a rough time of it. Haven't you, dearie? I'll tell you what I'm gonna do.

**NAOMI.** You'll place me under your protection?

**JUDITH.** I'll do better than that. I'll put you on the payroll. I could use a personal maid. The gal I have working for me now is… well…. Let's put it this way, she came with the house.

**ARGA.** I *heard* that.

**NAOMI.** Your personal maid? I've never had such an exalted position.

**ARGA.** Her position is usually doggie style.

**JUDITH.** Your duties would include running my bath, handling my wardrobe. I've got new gowns coming in all the time. I'm a perfect sample size.

**NAOMI.** That all sounds doable. Mistress, I promise not to betray your faith in me.

**JUDITH.** Well, then, glad to have you with the firm. I'll meet you back at the house.

**ARGA.** Such a vile creature entering our doors. I'll scrub the very portal with lye.

**NAOMI.** *(with angry vulgarity)* Scrub your pussy, old woman. *(suddenly catches herself and acts demure)* I'm sorry. That was uncalled for. Which house may it be?

**JUDITH.** Child, do you not know who I am? I am Judith, widow of Manasses.

**NAOMI.** Manazas?

**JUDITH.** Manasses, like Molasses. My home is the large fortress on the promontory. I'd give you a lift but I don't think the boys could handle a second passenger.

*(She turns to **THOR** who hands her a shawl that was draped on the litter)*

Cover your face with this pashmina and take the back roads. Those should be safe. I'll be there shortly.

**NAOMI.** Bless you. Bless you.

**JUDITH.** Child, I have not even asked, by what do they call thee?

**NAOMI.** Naomi. *(beat)* Naomi Beckerman.

*(**NAOMI** curtsies and runs off.)*

**JUDITH.** Poor kid.

**ARGA.** I still say a good stoning is what that girl needs.

**JUDITH.** Didja pick up them grapefruits?

**ARGA.** Yeah, I got 'em.

**JUDITH.** Well, hand 'em over. I'll take them home with me on my litter. No point in you shlepping them on your back.

*(**ARGA** gives her the bag of grapefruits. She's taken aback and confused by this act of generosity.)*

**ARGA.** That is most thoughtful of you, Mistress.

**JUDITH.** In an hour you'll forget it. *(she returns to the litter and sits)* Boys, I've finished my business here. Remove me to my home.

**CONAN.** Yes, Mistress. *(they lift her up)* Any particular route?

**JUDITH.** It looks like the sun is moving westward, and the workers will be returning from the fields, so take Jerusalem Road to the tunnel, exit on Moses, and then head straight up Macabee Drive.

**THOR.** Mistress, we shall be fleet of foot. Forward! March!

*(The men carry her off.)*

### END OF SCENE

## SCENE TWO

*(Judith's home. The room is marked by a tall arched
window that looks out on the city and the sea and sky.*
**ARGA** *enters followed by* **NAOMI**. *)*

**NAOMI.** Arga, I can barely breathe from anticipation of
news of a treaty.

**ARGA.** You'll need plenty of breath to complete your
household duties. I am too old to be doing everything
around here myself.

**NAOMI.** I completed all the tasks you've given me.

**ARGA.** You think so? I found a broken clasp on Mistress
Judith's velvet cloak, a scuff mark on her slipper, and a
loose thread on the coverlet. *(fiercely)* You deny it?

**NAOMI.** Enough already! I can't take any more of this
constant haranguing. I am not a professional
housekeeper. I am a former prostitute. My skills are
very specific. All I'm asking for is a little sympathy, a
little forbearance, some allowances maybe? But you
just keep coming at me, at me, at me, at me. You are
a total bitch. I've taken an informal poll. Uh huh, I
have, and except for the blind man, everyone in
Bethulia thinks of you with the affection they reserve
for a strain of the CLAP! *(catches herself)* I'm sorry. That
wasn't nice.

**ARGA.** *(very shaken)* Well, I can't help if I live by the high
standards established by my previous lady, the first wife
of Manasses.

**NAOMI.** *(trying to make things right)* You miss her, don't you?

**ARGA.** There are some who are unforgettable.

**NAOMI.** Tell me about her. Please.

**ARGA.** It pains me to tread the cold dank stones of
reminiscence. But how fondly I recall brushing my
lady's hair before she retired for the night. Five
hundred and thirty-seven strokes she'd say. And when
I finished with that precious task, I bathed her delicate
feet in rose water.

*(Unbeknownst to* **ARGA**, **JUDITH** *enters, holding something silken.)*

**ARGA**. She would then gently step out of her undergarments. And they were exquisite creations, as delicate as a spider's web and made from the finest and most loving of silk worms.

**JUDITH**. Arga, you've gotta live for today. Coincidentally, I just came across a *pair* of those old panties in a locked drawer. You want 'em?

*(***ARGA*** *violently grabs them out of* **JUDITH***'s hand.)*

**ARGA**. Give them to me! Now that you've touched them, I'll burn them.

**JUDITH**. Okay.

*(***ARGA*** *exits)*

**JUDITH**. There's always something rubbing her the wrong way. I can't seem to do anything right. I hope she's been treating you kindly.

**NAOMI**. We're getting used to each other's ways. Although today, she berated me for lining my eyes with kohl.

**JUDITH**. I *like* a smoky eye. Sometimes I add a drop of belladonna to make the pupils bigger. A tip I picked up from a catamite who was run out of town.

**NAOMI**. Your eyes are so beautiful. Never have I seen such long lashes.

**JUDITH**. I make them out of cock feathers and stick them on with corn syrup. When's your birthday? I'll make you a pair. Have you been happy here, my child?

**NAOMI**. Words cannot express my happiness. You have provided me with a safe haven, your friendship and the opportunity for rehabilitation.

**JUDITH**. And in time when you've regained your strength, I shall send you back into the world.

**NAOMI**. Please, don't. I beg of you. *(she gets on her knees, holding on to* **JUDITH***'s hand)* Don't send me back into the world of men! Grunting, hairy beasts of prey! Clawing me! Plundering me! Devouring me!

**JUDITH**. My dear one, I would be doing you a grave disservice if I allowed you to use my home as a permanent refuge. I harbor a dream, perhaps foolish, that one day you shall fall in love, marry and have children.

**NAOMI**. *(with dramatic intensity)* What man would ever want me, except as a tight hole in which to plunge his swollen member.

**JUDITH**. I think you're painting the picture rather bleak.

**NAOMI**. I'm just being realistic. Mistress Judith, I know you are far too young to be my mother.

**JUDITH**. *(sweetly)* You're right. I am.

**NAOMI**. You're barely of age to be my older sister.

**JUDITH**. You're right. I am.

**NAOMI**. Still, you have given me a mother's care. Why have you no children of your own?

**JUDITH**. I desperately longed for a child. Someone to love completely and selflessly. Alas, due to my husband's advanced years, Manasses could not perform the nocturnal duties of a husband. We traveled the world seeking advice from courtesans in Rome, concubines of the Orient, the Houri of India. Ah, the Houri. Great gals. You'd never think the Houri would be so funny. Antic. Belly laughs. But all their erotic suggestions were for naught. Still, I could not have loved the old man more.

**NAOMI**. And upon his death, you descended into a pit of deepest mourning.

**JUDITH**. But where most widows become black crows stripped of color; I expressed my grief in the acquisition of precious jewels, costly silken robes and shoes.

**NAOMI**. It pains me to imagine you suffering so.

**JUDITH**. My sufferings have been lessened by your presence, sweet child.

*(ARGA enters)*

**ARGA.** Mistress, there are soldiers surrounding the villa. Look out the window and see them below in the garden!

(**JUDITH** *and* **NAOMI** *rush to the window.*)

**NAOMI.** They're trampling your lovely peonies.

**JUDITH.** *(shouting below like a fishwife)* Hey! Get off of my flower beds! GET OUTTA THERE!!!

*(Ram's horns herald the entrance of General* **HOLOFERNES**, *in all of us military glory, accompanied* **URDAMANI** *and two soldiers.)*

**HOLOFERNES.** Mistress Judith, widow of Manasses, Do forgive the desecration of your verdant garden. My men have been at war too long and have lost their lightness of step.

**JUDITH.** We are grateful for the hope of a treaty. But here you are. There are others of far greater importance who anxiously await your august presence.

**HOLOFERNES.** The summit with the Bethulian Patriarchy can be delayed. I had to see you once more.

**JUDITH.** Once more? We have never met.

**HOLOFERNES.** Oh, but we have.

**JUDITH.** I don't think so. *(notices* **URDAMANI***)* But you look familiar.

**URDAMANI.** We met in the market place. I was posing as a woman.

**JUDITH.** That was you, huh? Very convincing. Y'ought to do it professionally.

**URDAMANI.** *(indignantly)* I am not a sluttish temple dancer. I am the Chief confidante of his supreme authority, Prince Holofernes.

**JUDITH.** I only meant I appreciate a skilled application of cosmetics. I seem to recall a most attractive lip stain.

**URDAMANI.** *(softening)* I mix the juices of both the raspberry and the pomegranate.

**JUDITH.** A pomegranate? Naomi, remember that.

**URDAMANI**. Throw in a little honey. It binds the pigments.

**HOLOFERNES**. My official business in Bethulia was predicated by –

**JUDITH**. What's the exact proportion of raspberry to pomegranate?

**URDAMANI**. It varies. If I want to go a little more pink, I'd suggest —

**HOLOFERNES**. Enough, Eunuch! Leave us be. And guards, you too remain outside the chamber.

**URDAMANI**. Yes, your most exalted.

**JUDITH**. Thanks for the tip, Tulip.

(**URDAMANI** *backs away and exits with the* **GUARDS**.)

**HOLOFERNES**. You are not repelled by my eunuch's effeminate ways?

**JUDITH**. I've always found the third sex to be most entertaining.

**HOLOFERNES**. Now, that I have dismissed my retinue, I must demand the same of you.

**JUDITH**. Girls, you may withdraw.

**ARGA**. Mistress, will you be safe?

**HOLOFERNES**. Your handmaiden regards me with distrust.

**ARGA**. Should I not distrust a hound of Lucifer?

**JUDITH**. Arga, please.

**HOLOFERNES**. Your face is a mask of disdain, and yet on closer inspection, you are still a fine specimen of your sex. Yes, a fine specimen.

**ARGA**. How dare you? I am a woman of impeccable virtue.

**HOLOFERNES**. A woman clings to her virtue as a snake does to its skin. In time both are sold.

**JUDITH**. I bet you made that one up yourself. Arga, feel free to carry forth your domestic duties.

**ARGA**. Yes, Mistress. Naomi, let's polish the credenza.

(*They exit.*)

**HOLOFERNES**. Your handmaiden has an adder's tongue that could bring disaster upon your household.

**JUDITH.** She's a character.

**HOLOFERNES.** You really do not recognize me, Mistress Judith? I was with my eunuch that day in the marketplace. I was disguised as a Jew.

**JUDITH.** So that was you.

**HOLOFERNES.** Have you no fear of the evil Holofernes?

**JUDITH.** The bull of Asshur. Have I reason to fear you?

**HOLOFERNES.** Thousands do, but perhaps it is I who should fear you. Great beauty can be a weapon as mighty as the sharpest blade. And you have quite an arsenal.

**JUDITH.** Kindly keep your eyes off my arsenal.

**HOLOFERNES.** It's been too long since I've luxuriated in the company of women. I'm really quite intoxicated.

**JUDITH.** So you like women.

**HOLOFERNES.** *(intrigued)* You bet I do. Men are such inferior beings.

**JUDITH.** That's rather harsh.

**HOLOFERNES.** How easily they can be fed false hopes. The thrill I receive from the butchery of my foes is only exceeded by my delight in toying with their minds.

**JUDITH.** Are you implying that you have no intention of negotiating a treaty?

**HOLOFERNES.** Unlike your foolish patriarchy, you are a being of some intelligence.

**JUDITH.** And you're despicable.

**HOLOFERNES.** *(sniffing)* Ah, the aromatic sweetness of your sex.

**JUDITH.** Now it's all becoming crystal clear. You came to Bethulia today for one reason and one reason only, to sniff at my nether regions.

**HOLOFERNES.** Grant me what I desire and your people shall reap the benefit.

**JUDITH.** Only a fool would believe a word you'd say.

**HOLOFERNES.** You shall bitterly regret thwarting my desires.

**JUDITH.** And thwart 'em I shall. Now take your soldiers, your eunuch, your nasal passages and get outta here.

*(There is a commotion outside,* **URDAMANI** *enters followed by the two* **GUARDS** *who are dragging in our narrator,* **NATHAN**. **ARGA** *and* **NAOMI**, *concerned, follow them into the room.)*

**NATHAN**. Let go of me! Let go of me!

**HOLOFERNES**. What is this?

**URDAMANI**. General, we discovered this assassin lurking in the shadows. He was hiding a weapon.

**NATHAN**. That is not true! Let me go!

**HOLOFERNES**. You are not acting alone. I can *smell* your fear.

**JUDITH**. Yeah. So can a cocker spaniel.

**HOLOFERNES**. Who are your confederates? Speak, boy, or I shall carve the truth upon your smooth cheek.

**JUDITH**. Bagoas, you are late again

**HOLOFERNES**. You know this youth?

**JUDITH**. He is a sculptor. I commissioned him to carve a marble bust of me. I was less than satisfied with the smile.

**URDAMANI**. She's lying.

**ARGA**. How dare you impugn my mistress!

**JUDITH**. Thanks, Arga.

**HOLOFERNES**. You are then a sculptor?

**NATHAN**. Yes, I am.

**HOLOFERNES**. Rather young for such an important commission.

**NATHAN**. I have been till now a mere apprentice.

**URDAMANI**. And what of the weapon in your possession?

**NATHAN**. It is a chisel I employ in my work.

**JUDITH**. You may view the bust in progress, if you so wish, General.

**HOLOFERNES**. That would be a disappointment if the smile was not captured. We shall leave him to his artistic challenge. And return at once to camp!

**ARGA**. But what of the treaty?

**HOLOFERNES**. I have achieved all I intended from my visit. Henceforth, Bethulia *(with an unavoidable lisp)* will see the scabrous side of my saber. *(catches himself)* Men! Away!

 *(**HOLOFERNES**, **URDAMANI** and the two **GUARDS** exit. **NATHAN** nearly collapses from relief.)*

**JUDITH**. You little fool. Who are you? Did you think you could simply march in here and assassinate the General?

**NATHAN**. I did what I must. I did what any man of honor should do?

**ARGA**. You endangered all of our lives

**NATHAN**. Your lives are endangered as long as he lives.

**NAOMI**. What is your name, boy?

**NATHAN**. They call me Nathan. Mistress Judith, when you gave me the profession of sculptor, you were not far off the mark. I am a poet. But in a mad world, the poet must employ a dagger as well as words.

**NAOMI**. Your arm is scratched.

**NATHAN**. A wound. My flesh forever scarred like the very land itself.

**NAOMI**. *(amused)* Silly boy. Here. I shall take proper care of you as a mother would.

 *(She takes a rag off her waist, spits on it and wipes the blood off his arm.)*

**NATHAN**. Mock me again, fair one, for your gay laughter is like a brook when it trips and falls over stones on its way.

**NAOMI**. These brutal days have little call for laughter. But one cannot resist a fool.

**NATHAN**. I am a fool and your touch is gentle.

 *(**JUDITH** is amused by their very clear chemistry.)*

**JUDITH**. Arga, the young man will be staying for luncheon.

**ARGA**. But we have no food to spare. The larder is nearly empty.

**JUDITH**. Oh, I'm sure you can rustle up something both delicious and nutritious.

**ARGA**. I'll make a tabouli.

**JUDITH**. I'll help you.

**ARGA**. *(whispering)* But we mustn't leave them alone. He's a good looking young man with a young man's healthy appetites and she's a barely reformed ex— . She might fall back on her old ways.

**JUDITH**. Arga, the tomatoes. Let's peel 'em.

(**JUDITH** *pushes* **ARGA** *out of the room. They exit.*)

**NATHAN**. I am glad they left.

**NAOMI**. You are impertinent.

**NATHAN**. I am bedazzled.

**NAOMI**. So you are a poet. I am in awe of talent. I possess no talents. Skills, but no talents.

**NATHAN**. You have the gift of tenderness.

*(She finishes bandaging his wrist.)*

**NAOMI**. If it is a gift, it is one I long to share.

*(They embrace. She pulls apart.)*

I shouldn't have done that. It was wrong. Shameful.

**NATHAN**. But why?

**NAOMI**. You don't know me. I can see by your unblemished face that you are good and pure. I doubt you would even recognize corruption in others.

**NATHAN**. I see in your features a trusting soul yearning for affection. I know I am but a callow youth with no past amorous conquests. Allow me to give you a virgin's kiss.

**NAOMI**. Oh, but I'm – I'm – If you only knew the truth about me, you would flee for shelter in the nearest Shul.

**NATHAN**. But I do know of you.

**NAOMI**. *(suddenly tough and suspicious)* What have you heard?

**NATHAN**. That your fragile beauty has been trampled, exploited and abused by a legion of heartless brutes.

**NAOMI**. I wouldn't say a legion, but – yeah, it's been a legion.

**NATHAN**. And yet your eyes reveal an eternal innocence from which I may nearly swoon.

**NAOMI**. So many words.

**NATHAN**. Of my gentle ways you needn't fear or worry. Only chicks and ducks and geese better scurry.

**NAOMI**. A torrent of beautiful words. Oh, I swore to my Mistress on the graves of my ancestors, that I would be good. Please, I beg of you. Leave me to my vow.

**NATHAN**. You cannot cast me off.

**NAOMI**. Then, come back tomorrow, when I've had time to think.

**NATHAN**. Tomorrow is an indulgence we can ill afford, for there very well may not be a future.

**NAOMI**. There must be a tomorrow. It would be too cruel for God to give us but this solitary moment.

*(They kiss).*

**NATHAN**. Your eyes are at once free of torment.

**NAOMI**. It is a miracle, for I feel no shame, my darling sweet Nathan.

**NATHAN**. You speak my name as it has never been spoken. Seraphim of my dreams, what do I call thee?

**NAOMI**. Naomi. Naomi Beckerman.

### END OF SCENE

## SCENE THREE

*(***NATHAN*** *narrates.)*

**NATHAN**. Naomi Beckerman. Naomi Beckerman. Each enchanting syllable floated above my head like a silvery planet from the heavens. I pledged that upon the fall of the Assyrians, I, Nathan, would spend the rest of my life, composing odes to her ethereal beauty. But would I – would any of us live to see a world of peace. When Judith spurned the General, he took his revenge by further persecuting the citizens of Bethulia. His campaign against us was hindered by the terror he struck in the hearts of his own captains.

*(Lights down on ***NATHAN*** and up on ***HOLOFERNES***. A masked Assyrian ***CAPTAIN***, arms bound, is thrust onto the stage. He falls to his knees.)*

**HOLOFERNES**. You dare come to me with news of defeat! Captain, you shall pay for this with the loss of a hand. Which one shall I sever? I am merciful. It shall be your choice.

**CAPTAIN**. General, do you not see that your captains would rather lose their lives in battle and leave the Bethulians free, than risk your displeasure with reports of failure?

**HOLOFERNES**. You dare criticize me? Both hands shall be mine to be used as back scratchers! Away with you to the chopping block!

*(The ***CAPTAIN*** hobbles off screaming, followed by ***HOLOFERNES***. Lights up on ***NATHAN***.)*

**NATHAN**. One night during the siege, I met with my companions below in the Widow's moonlit garden.

*(Two young men, ***SIMON*** and ***OZIAS***, join ***NATHAN***.)*

Hunger, thirst and fever rule us now. Starvation draws nearer each day. But there is always hope, which fills me with the lightness of a hummingbird flitting to the highest branch. We have still some grain, and just outside the Eastern Gate there is a spring the foe have not yet discovered.

**OZIAS.** Nathan, I have learned this very night our enemies have crept up to the outer wall and dammed that precious source of water.

**SIMON.** Our men did their best to protect the wells, but now the bodies of our comrades choke the stream.

**NATHAN.** Even with this grim dispatch, my spirit remains buoyant as a leaping dolphin. Our people have strength to spare.

**OZIAS.** Nathan, at set of sun two women and a child were taken with a strange sickness on the street.

**SIMON.** Perchance they drank of some infected well. It will soon be a plague.

**NATHAN.** *(in agony)* You both plague *me* with each fresh calamity! Everything conspires to drag me down into a quagmire of despair.

**OZIAS.** There is no one to help us. No one! No one!

**SIMON.** All are cowards. Their sufferings have made them selfish.

**NATHAN.** Only one has risen from her fear. Dead Manasses wife. Judith.

**OZIAS.** *(clearly besotted)* Ah, Judith!

**SIMON.** What? The wealthy widow who resides in this grand tower high above our heads? She who is mocked for her craving for luxury? *She* who is known to squander a thousand silver talents on a mere bagatelle?

**NATHAN.** Yes, that is she. But they do not know the real woman. Through the siege her touch has soothed the dying, and her voice in their ears whispers hope.

**OZIAS.** *(in his own reverie)* Judith! Whisper in *my* ear!

**SIMON.** Are we talking about the same Judith? The redhead with the cocksucker lips?

**OZIAS.** Indeed. Her flame colored tresses have been seen in every dingy by-way of the town where grief or pain has built its abode. Judith!

NATHAN. No hovel is too loathsome that the door-sill does not bear her sandal-print. Ah, here she comes. We must not let her see us.

*(The three boys hide in the shadows.* JUDITH *drags a small cart full of groceries. A dark, hobbled figure of a man enters, his face covered by a shawl, and looks furtively around.)*

JUDITH. Come quickly. I have filled the cart with barley, potatoes and a nice, thick Porterhouse.

MAN. A porterhouse?

JUDITH. Aged and marbled.

MAN. Blessed lady, once again you have saved my family from starvation

JUDITH. Do not thank me. I would gladly tear the jewels from my neck if your family could eat them. It's a sad commentary when a dozen grains of barley are worth more than a rajah's pearl. Here, quickly, return to your home before anyone sees us.

*(The man weakened by starvation, tries to pull the wagon but stumbles.)*

MAN. Forgive me. I shall be on my way.

JUDITH. What a fool I am. You are too weak from famine to pull this freight. I shall be your cart horse and deliver your groceries.

*(*JUDITH *pushes the cart off stage, and is followed by the poor man. The boys come out of the shadows.)*

SIMON. My eyes betray me! The lady is an angel of mercy! Curse me for believing the vile rumors that so unfairly cling to her name.

OZIAS. Blessed Judith! The divine Judith! Judy!

SIMON. The people must be told that such a pure soul walks among them.

NATHAN. No, Simon. We must never speak of the beneficence we've witnessed this night. The poor may think of her as a prophetess but the widow keeps her good work a secret among her own class, lo they spit on her as a second wife who profited from her dead husband's fortune. I hear someone! Reach for your daggers!

(**ARGA** *finds them. She's carrying a small sack.*)

**ARGA.** Nathan, it is only I, Arga. *(to* **OZIAS***)* You I know. Ozias. Your mother works for the Resnicks down the hill. *(to* **SIMON***)* But who is *this* young man?

**SIMON.** I am Simon, friend to Nathan and to all who will die for freedom.

**ARGA.** You have a good face. Sensitive eyes. Nathan, I've filled a satchel full of yams, rutabagas and sandwich meats. Deliver them among the needy. I would take more from our cellar but I don't want my mistress to become suspicious. As everyone knows, she's an utterly selfish creature, with no regard for the sufferings of others.

(*The boys look to each other with sage knowledge of* **JUDITH***'s goodness.*)

**NATHAN.** So we've heard.

**ARGA.** Strangely, much of our food is missing. It must be vandals. But who can blame them in these desperate times. So tell me, what's going on? I may be a woman but I'm a tough old bird who can slice up an Assyrian soldier as well as I can butcher a side of beef.

**SIMON.** We are a small ragtag army of beardless youths and we accept your offer gladly.

**ARGA.** Dare I say, I may have more facial hair than *any* of you.

**NATHAN.** *(joking)* Not so, my good woman. I have the beginnings of a most distinguished moustache.

**OZIAS.** Yes, and he darkens it with beet juice.

(*The boys all laugh and jostle each other in the bawdy Shakespearean manner.*)

**SIMON.** What right have you to jest, Ozias, ye who have sprouted nary a sign of down on your peach-like countenance.

**OZIAS**. Perhaps so, but I have seen the growth of a dense foliage surrounding my most august of mighty trees.

**NATHAN**. A tree? At best a root vegetable. Be it parsnip or squash?

**SIMON**. Methinks radish!

*(The three boys roughhouse.)*

**ARGA**. Shhhhh. Cease at once this jocular hooting. You'll awaken my mistress from her selfish slumber. Now *I* hear someone.

*(**NAOMI** comes out of the shadows.)*

**NAOMI**. It is only I, Naomi Lynn Beckerman.

**NATHAN**. My love, you shouldn't be out here after the curfew. Softer than starlight are you. Warmer than winds of June are the gentle lips you gave me.

**NAOMI**. Thank you, but I bring news that could alter the very destiny of our beleaguered Bethulia.

**ARGA**. You?

**NAOMI**. This afternoon I was running an errand for my mistress when I ran into a former colleague um friend of mine. Her name is Ruby.

**ARGA**. Naomi, how many times have I told you, it is imperative that you never associate with that kind of woman.

**NATHAN**. Arga, let her speak.

**NAOMI**. Ruby told me that she was intimately acquainted with a Captain; a most trusted lieutenant of General Holofernes, who goes by the name of Lamech. What the evil General doesn't know is that Lamech holds a secret deep within his breast. He is a Jew.

**SIMON**. What a stroke of fortune!

**OZIAS**. Too good to be true!

**NATHAN**. We must get word to this guard. Can your friend be trusted to carry forth a missive?

**NAOMI**. Unfortunately not. Ruby is a decent soul but like most of the population; frozen in terror.

**ARGA.** All right. Gather round. This is what we're gonna do. I'll bake a challah. We'll insert a message within the dough and have it delivered to the trusted Captain by means of a daisy chain. One link must never know the identity of the one two steps ahead.

**NATHAN.** Your plan leaves much room for failure.

**ARGA.** I'm telling you, it's fool proof.

**NAOMI.** Nathan is right. There can be only one courier. Someone the enemy could not possibly view as a threat. I shall be that courier.

**ARGA.** Oh, no.

**OZIAS.** This mere slip of a girl?

**NATHAN.** I could not allow it. You would be sacrificing your life.

**NAOMI.** You must not deny me my great chance for redemption.

**SIMON.** Redemption? Why should you, fair maiden, seek redemption?

**ARGA.** *(nervously)* We can um discuss this further tomorrow.

**SIMON.** *(Suddenly recognizing* **NAOMI***)* We've met before. When first Nathan introduced us, I felt that we had some earlier acquaintance, but could not remember when.

**NATHAN.** I doubt that is possible.

**SIMON.** But now, at last, all is clear! You dear sweet soul. I am forever in your debt.

**NAOMI.** *(sincerely)* I'm afraid I don't remember you.

**SIMON.** I was but twelve years old. Twas my birthday and my hideous bully of a stepfather arranged for me to lose my virginity on that very night. My clothes were stripped from me and I was thrust into a dark room with my stepfather's drunken cronies jeering from without. Inside was a young girl, nearly my own age and hired for the evening's festivities. She wiped away my tears and with the most supreme patience and gentleness, initiated me into premature manhood. I was never able to properly thank her. I thank her now.

*(He kisses her hand.* **NATHAN** *freezes.)*

**NATHAN**. Simon, you have mistaken my Naomi for some creature of the shadows.

**SIMON**. I swear upon my life that I am in the presence of she who hath made me complete.

**ARGA**. *(trying to cover up this mess)* Naomi is a pretty girl but she has a Semitic look very common to these parts.

**NATHAN**. Take back those words! I demand it!

**OZIAS**. Simon meant no disrespect.

**NATHAN**. Take them back, I say!

**SIMON**. My crime is only speaking the truth!

**NAOMI**. *(simply)* He speaks the truth. I am that girl.

**ARGA**. Now, it's all out.

**SIMON**. Friend, I meant no harm.

**OZIAS**. Naomi, of the three of us, only I remain a virgin. Could you possibly see it in your heart to—

**NATHAN**. *(in agony)* No! My patience is being tested in ways that no man could ever accept!

**NAOMI**. My love, complete honesty is our only hope.

**NATHAN**. Do not speak to me!

**ARGA**. Stop this, Nathan! You had no illusions about her purity. You know well the life she led.

**NATHAN**. But spreading her legs for my bosom friend!

**SIMON**. I have only provided further proof of her goodness of spirit.

**NAOMI**. Nathan, please, do not forsake me.

**OZIAS**. You must forgive her.

**ARGA**. Nathan, lissen to me. This is the opportunity for you to go from boy to man. Seize it. Come Simon. Come, Ozias. We must leave them be. Nathan, be wise.

*(***ARGA*** *exits with* **SIMON** *and* **OZIAS***)*

**NAOMI**. Nathan, this was bound to happen. Let's face it. I got around. *(resigned)* So then it's over. Love vanquished. I was a fool to think happiness could ever be mine.

*(Sadly, she begins to walk away.* **NATHAN** *stops her.)*

**NATHAN.** Don't go!

*(She stops.)*

You must forgive me for losing my head. Angel and lover, heaven and earth. Perhaps it's a wondrous chance that I can benefit from your worldly experience. And I have my poetry to share with *you*. We can both be teacher and student.

**NAOMI.** There is so much that I can learn from you.

**NATHAN.** Yes. Your heart remains that of a child; protected as if in a precious shell. Never to be sullied.

**NAOMI.** Any act of perversity was endured by this other girl, who has ceased to exist. It was that other Naomi who was taught by cruel masters the sensual arts of decadent pleasure.

**NATHAN.** Yes, the other Naomi.

**NAOMI.** That unfortunate girl learned very well how to "ride the chariot."

**NATHAN.** The poor darling.

**NAOMI.** Then there was this degrading position we used to call "spreading the peacock tail."

**NATHAN.** Never heard of that.

**NAOMI.** And "rowing the barge," "the double sphinx." "The butter churn."

**NATHAN.** Stop it! Stop it! I can bear no more! I am tortured by these visions! Even in this dim moonlight, I can see finger marks of the countless men who have touched you.

**NAOMI.** Nathan, don't say such a thing!

**NATHAN.** I wish I could kill every man you pleasured.

**NAOMI.** You are really something. You are *really* something. Where do you get off expressing rage? You have no excuse for rage. Not until you've earned your living on your back. Then come to me and say you're full of rage. See this face! This is the face of bitterness. All of the lines are going downward. A deep furrow etched between my eyes bespeaks of my torment. I have pouches and jowls bloated with the bile of resentment. But even my bitterness cannot compare with the ugliness that jealousy has made of your features.

NATHAN. I can't help it. You ask too much!

(*NATHAN runs off into the night.* NAOMI *is left alone, hopeless.*)

NAOMI. I have asked too much of God. Devoid of future, my life is now expendable. I shall be the courier and damn the consequences! From now on, it's the Assyrian army versus Naomi Lynn Barbara Beckerman!

## END OF SCENE

## SCENE FOUR

*(The enemy camp.* **HOLOFERNES** *enters, followed by* **URDAMANI**. **HOLOFERNES** *is examining a scrolled map of the region.)*

**HOLOFERNES.** The city of Bethulia should have been leveled to dust long ago. Damn my Captains for their incompetence!

**URDAMANI.** Your sublime eminence, dare I say you seem rather out of sorts today.

**HOLOFERNES.** Yes, Urdamani, I am out of sorts. Y'ever have those days when you've ordered all of your executions, had a dozen subservients impaled on spikes and yet nothing seems to be going your way.

**URDAMANI.** Master, you're a perfectionist. It's both a blessing and a curse. What can I do to ease your stress? A massage? A head to toe massage? I'll start by cooling your feverish brow with unguents. And then slooooowly work my way down.

**HOLOFERNES.** How repulsed I am by your soft, moist fingers. If I am to be touched in my most intimate regions, it should be by an enslaved woman, not an infatuated gelding.

**URDAMANI.** I was only trying to please, your excellency.

**HOLOFERNES.** You disgust me.

*(A hooded* **CAPTAIN #2** *enters the tent.)*

**CAPTAIN #2.** Your excellency.

**HOLOFERNES.** Yes, Captain.

**CAPTAIN #2.** A young girl, a prostitute, has been captured attempting to pass through the Eastern Gate. There is every suspicion that she is a spy.

**HOLOFERNES.** A spying prostitute. The day is improving. Let us entertain ourselves with the girl.

*(They exit.)*

## END OF SCENE

## SCENE FIVE

*(Judith's home. The following day.* **JUDITH** *and* **ARGA** *are both frantic with worry.)*

**JUDITH.** What did you say to her?

**ARGA.** What do you mean, what did I say to her?

**JUDITH.** Well, Naomi is missing. She probably ran off because you berated her for some domestic trifle. Nothing she could ever do was right.

**ARGA.** I was extremely fond of that girl, and devoted to her rehabilitation.

**JUDITH.** Well, it couldn't have been anything I said.

**ARGA.** *(making a big decision)* Mistress Judith, we didn't want you to know but….

**JUDITH.** We? Who's we?

**ARGA.** Nathan and his partisans. Naomi was sent on a mission.

**JUDITH.** A mission? What kind of mission?

**ARGA.** She was sent to penetrate the enemy camp.

**JUDITH.** Naomi? Penetration? Camp?

**ARGA.** Her goal was to deliver a message to a Captain of Holofernes who is said to be a closet Jew. She's a determined young lady. She could very well be on her way back home.

**JUDITH.** I think you're being extremely cavalier.

*(A din is heard outside the chamber.* **NATHAN** *and* **OZIAS** *enter holding up Simon, who has been ravaged by the enemy forces.)*

**NATHAN.** We need help!

**JUDITH.** What has happened?

**OZIAS.** Simon climbed over the wall. A child needed water and he was determined to be of aid. Enemy soldiers caught him and would have torn him to shreds, had they not been distracted by a ship coming into port.

**ARGA.** Let's lie him down.

*(They move him over to the divan.)*

**SIMON.** Before I was attacked, I received news of.... of........

**JUDITH.** Of who? Do you have news of Naomi?

**SIMON.** Yes.... Naomi.

**NATHAN.** What of Naomi? Is she safe? Where is she now?

**SIMON.** She is dead. She never reached the enemy camp. I am told she was seized and immediately decapitated on the far side of the Valley of the lepers.

**ARGA.** That poor girl.

**NATHAN.** My angel Naomi!

**JUDITH.** A daughter.

*(**NATHAN** removes from the pouch draped around his torso, a small vial.)*

**ARGA.** Nathan, what have you there?

**NATHAN.** A vial of poison. Enough to join my beloved. I cannot live without my love.

**JUDITH.** Give that to me, you foolish boy.

**NATHAN.** Naomi, smile at me once more!

*(He dashes out of the room.)*

**JUDITH.** Nathan!

*(They all chase after **NATHAN**.)*


## END OF SCENE

## SCENE SIX

*(The enemy camp.* **HOLOFERNES** *enters, followed by* **URDAMANI***, who in turns is followed by* **CAPTAIN #2** *who has Naomi, bound and gagged, thrown over his shoulder. He places her on her feet as if she were a bound rug.)*

**HOLOFERNES.** My, how scrumptiously vulnerable you are. As helpless as a bound rug. And when I so desire, I will unbound and trample on you as easily as I would tread an Oriental, sissle or shag. Captain, unbind the prostitute.

*(The* **CAPTAIN** *is about to remove the rope that binds her, but* **URDAMANI** *stops him.)*

**URDAMANI.** General, allow me to prepare the captive for you.

**HOLOFERNES.** Prepare?

**URDAMANI.** Yes. She is clearly of the streets. Allow me to bathe and delouse her for your pleasure.

**HOLOFERNES.** Perhaps you're right, Urdamani. And how kind we shall be. She will die thoroughly cleansed, if not in soul than in body. Come, Captain. Let us leave the Eunuch to his filthy chore.

*(***HOLOFERNES** *and the* **CAPTAIN** *exit.)*

**URDAMANI.** Child, you see that I and I alone have kept you from harm's way. The General will stop at nothing to force a confession from you. I have delayed your torment for I– I am in need of a confessor. A silent witness to my pain. Holofernes. Demon! Malignant spirit from Hell! Damn you for torturing me! I was brought into the General's service years ago as a mere water boy. You should have seen me then; a lad of extraordinary beauty. It's only in recent years that I've developed a bit of a weight problem. I just need to cut out sweets. In those early days, I was content to polish the General's weapons and bring him much needed beverage on the field of battle. As time marched on, I craved more. I longed to be his intimate servant. However, the only men allowed to bathe him were eunuchs. I fought the battle raging within me. Genitalia or bathing the General. Genitalia or bathing the General. How do you choose? There was no choice. I made the cut myself. In a blood ceremony upon a holy alter I presented that despised flesh to my warrior Prince. At long last, his body was mine. However, to my horror, I learned that groveling servitude would not satisfy my craving. Holofernes, why do you torment me so? Fiend! Incubus! My sacrifice has left me with a mound as bare as the vast desert, with no oasis to provide pleasure. I've an uncontrollable itch to scratch. I, who possess neither penis nor snatch.

*(He rubs his body against the helpless* **NAOMI**.*)*

**URDAMANI**. Holofernes, my evil Prince, tickle my mound. That's all I ask. At least, give me that! Give me that! Tickle my mound!

*(***URDAMANI*** *suddenly becomes aware of* **NAOMI***'s presence. He turns vicious.)*

Girl, your eyes betray your contempt and worse, your pity. Guard! Take her away!!!

*(The* **GUARD** *returns, picks up* **NAOMI** *and carries her off.)*

*(wistfully)* Holofernes, tickle my mound.

*(He exits.)*

## END OF SCENE

## SCENE SEVEN

(JUDITH's *home, a few minutes after we last saw them.* NATHAN *enters followed by* JUDITH, ARGA, *Simon and* OZIAS.)

NATHAN. Mistress Judith, how dare you empty my vial of poison. How dare you deny me my reunion with my dead love.

JUDITH. Too many of our fair flowers have been cut down before they've blossomed.

SIMON. We are hardly budding roses. I am nothing but a useless stem of ragweed.

OZIAS. And I, a skunk cabbage.

ARGA. Poor Naomi. I was wrong to have judged her so harshly. A few simple words of encouragement would have meant so much. I shall curse myself to the end of my days.

NATHAN. *(impassioned)* We are all cursed! God, I accept our destruction! I see now that it was your divine plan for us to be defeated.

OZIAS. One can't fight God's will.

SIMON. We are in his power.

JUDITH. *(outraged)* God's will? Holofernes is the instrument of God? Naomi was meant to die? What gibberish you speak!

NATHAN. There is a divine purpose to everything in the world. We must abandon ourselves to his better judgment.

JUDITH. If I abandoned myself to God's plan, I'd still be picking up towels in the baths. God helps those who help themselves.

ARGA. You can't argue with that.

JUDITH. We who are unable to plumb the depths of the human heart or grasp the way the mind works, how can we presume to understand the Maker of mortal beings?

**ARGA.** I'm with her on that one.

**NATHAN.** So all is a grand mystery? God has no greater plan for us? Your words do nothing to inspire me. Good gentlemen, let us return to our homes and await the inevitable. *(He removes another small vial from the leather pouch at his waist.)* I have with me another vial; a delicate though powerful potion, culled from fennel, rue and rosemary, that provides a drowsy calm. I shall take it moments before I stab myself.

*(ARGA grabs it out of his hand.)*

**ARGA.** I will not hear such foolish talk.

**NATHAN.** Consider it a gift, Arga. You will need it when the Assyrian forces invade this house.

*(NATHAN and OZIAS lift SIMON off of the divan.)*

**SIMON.** Fair Widow, forgive us our weakness.

**OZIAS.** We are, alas, but boys.

**NATHAN.** Gentle Naomi, we shall soon be with thee.

*(They leave.)*

**ARGA.** With them goes our last hope. It will not be long before we are all made slaves and put to death. Strengthen me, O God of Jerusalem!

*(JUDITH begins to feel an unearthly presence.)*

**JUDITH.** My heart pounds. My head is light.

**ARGA.** Come, Lady. Let me escort you to your bed chamber.

**JUDITH.** *(to unseen voices)* I cannot understand you.

**ARGA.** I said, let me escort you to your bed chamber.

**JUDITH.** Not you. Them.

**ARGA.** Them? Oh, no. Now what.

**JUDITH.** I seem to hear weird voices round me, words shaped and uttered by invisible lips.

**ARGA.** My lady has gone mad.

**JUDITH.** See you not a white hand that with its leveled finger points through the air?

**ARGA.** Nought but the vacant air do I behold.

**JUDITH**. There! It still lingers, like a silver mist!

**ARGA**. *(to herself)* She seems like one inspired – mark her brow, the radiance of it!

**JUDITH**. T'is gone! Fear not; it was a sign to me alone. The finger pointed in the direction of the Eastern gate!

**ARGA**. The finger?

**JUDITH**. The finger. It pointed to the Eastern gate, on the other side of which lies the enemy camp. Shield me with thy prayers. Thither I go.

**ARGA**. O Mistress, what your purpose is, I do not know. I see only this, in yonder camp, among those barbarous hordes, swift death awaits you.

*(**ARGA** grabs her wrist.)*

**JUDITH**. Arga, free my wrist! Naught shall bar my way.

**ARGA**. If you insist upon embarking on this mysterious errand, I shall go with you.

**JUDITH**. No. Our path divides here. I must prepare for the journey. I shall go richly decked, pearls in my hair and diamonds on my bosom. I shall drape myself in the gown that has lain unworn since I was wed.

**ARGA**. Your wedding gown. Some thought it magnificent. Others found it skirted bad taste. I confess I was among the latter. But regardless, I must follow thee.

**JUDITH**. No, Arga. I go to free my people, and gladly pay for it with my life.

**ARGA**. How do you a lone fragile woman intend to free our people?

**JUDITH**. By freeing the head of Holofernes from his body.

*(music cue)*

**ARGA**. Oh, no!

**JUDITH**. I shall require some reliquary or casket. What have we in the house large enough to contain a General's head?

**ARGA**. *(the truth dawning on her)* This is not your first selfless act. It is *you* who have been emptying our cellar of food.

**JUDITH**. Speak not another word.

**ARGA**. *You* are the angel of mercy that the poor and suffering speak of with such adoration. More blind than old Mordechai have I been! More foolish than Essie the feeble minded. I beseech thee, Mistress. Forgive me for not seeing you as you are, that most noble of women.

**JUDITH**. My dear Arga, of course you are forgiven. Say nothing more. Destiny calls. I must dress for battle. The gown may need alterations.

(**JUDITH** *slowly exits as* **ARGA**, *hands in ecstatic prayer, watches her Mistress leave for her destiny. Inspirational music builds to a crescendo as* **ARGA** *follows her mistress.*

**END OF SCENE**

## SCENE EIGHT

*(A street in Bethulia.* **NATHAN** *enters. From the other side of the stage he is met by Simon and* **OZIAS**.*)*

**OZIAS.** Simon, there he is!

**SIMON.** Nathan!

**NATHAN.** What are you both doing on the streets? The patriarchs have issued a strict curfew.

**SIMON.** Nathan, my mother sent me to find Arga. My grandmother Hanne Leah is ill. But the house of Manasses is dark and no one appears to be within.

**NATHAN.** In this time of hopelessness, no doubt Mistress Judith and her servants have taken to their beds.

**OZIAS.** The silversmith told us that he saw Mistress Judith and Arga walking with great purpose towards the hill.

**SIMON.** And the crippled seamstress, Paulina, says she saw from her window the women approaching the Eastern Gate.

**OZIAS.** The old blind man Mordechai told us that he heard the two women reach the Gate, and Arga pleading with her Mistress to turn back.

**SIMON.** Josiah, the cross eyed tailor saw from his roof the two women stopped by soldiers. After a brief contretemps, the women were escorted through the gate. I fear that they will never been seen again.

**NATHAN.** I can only assume they are in search of some word of my dead beloved. God, why should you take first my Naomi, and now Judith, that most generous of beings.

**OZIAS.** And Arga.

**NATHAN.** Oh yes, her too. My friends, come join me in mournful prayer. *(The three young men exit.)*

## END OF SCENE

## SCENE NINE

*(The enemy camp of* **HOLOFERNES**. *A* **CAPTAIN** *pushes* **NAOMI** *into the tent. Her arms are tied but there is no restraint in her mouth. They are followed by* **HOLOFERNES** *and* **URDAMANI**.*)*

**NAOMI**. *(defiantly)* Torture me all you want. My spirit shall not be broken.

**HOLOFERNES**. We are all broken in time. Only a child would believe otherwise. My dear, good fortune has smiled on you. I have chosen to be merciful.

**NAOMI**. You will return me to my people?

**HOLOFERNES**. Unfortunately, no. You are to be sent on a slave ship along with my other spoils of war to Macedonia. Laborers are needed. Your short life will be one of unbearable hardship, but I have given you several years more to worship your invisible God. You might thank me for my bounty.

**NAOMI**. I offer you no thanks, you sick freak. Would I thank a weasel? Would I thank a parasite? Would I thank a parasite embedded in a beggar woman's feces? I spit on you is what I do!

**HOLOFERNES**. Ungrateful harlot! *(He slaps her.)* Take her away!

*(The* **CAPTAIN** *pushes her out of the tent.)*

**NAOMI**. You cannot silence the truuuuuuuth!!!!

*(They exit.)*

**HOLOFERNES**. My acts of charity are never appreciated.

**URDAMANI**. I have always considered you, General, the most benevolent of earthly beings.

**HOLOFERNES**. And you, alone, ask so little of me, faithful Urdamani.

**URDAMANI**. Your most exalted, there *is* something that you could do for me.

**HOLOFERNES**. Speak, pray. It would please me, Urdamani, to give you some small kindness.

**URDAMANI.** I should like the return of my genitalia.

**HOLOFERNES.** *(at a loss)* Your genitalia? I have in my possession your genitalia?

**URDAMANI.** Certainly you must recall that years ago when I made the ultimate sacrifice in being your servant, I presented you with the gift of my severed organs.

**HOLOFERNES.** Really?

**URDAMANI.** You had them pickled in brine and preserved in a turquoise and gold casket. It would give me great satisfaction to have them returned.

**HOLOFERNES.** Yes. It's all coming back to me. Oh yes. A perfectly respectable set of genitals. But returning them is quite out of the question.

**URDAMANI.** Out of the question, my Lord?

**HOLOFERNES.** Years ago, I presented that jeweled casket as a gift to a beautiful and hopelessly virginal noblewoman I was bent on deflowering. The pitiful human flesh within the casket was tossed to my dogs. Urdamani, you must relieve yourself of foolish sentimentality. It is really quite useless. Come, Eunuch, my toenails need attention.

*(***HOLOFERNES*** exits. ***URDAMANI***, devastated, at long last sees ***HOLOFERNES*** for the monster he is.)*

**URDAMANI.** I asked for so little. So little.

*(He exits in Holofernes' direction. ***JUDITH*** and ***ARGA*** enter from the other side of the stage. ***JUDITH*** glitters in a fabulous gold gown and jeweled turban. ***ARGA*** is carrying a wig box.)*

**JUDITH.** For an army tent, the General certainly doesn't stint on luxury. Such riches.

**ARGA.** And all pilfered. See that gold chamber pot? Stolen from the Widow Lazar.

**JUDITH.** How do you like that. I thought it looked familiar. I've sat on that commode.

*(Two ***CAPTAINS*** enter.)*

CAPTAIN. Who are ye that trespass?

ARGA. I accompany my mistress, Judith of Bethulia, the widow of Manasses.

CAPTAIN. Repeat the name?

*(He unrolls a small scroll and searches for the name.)*

JUDITH. Manasses like Molasses.

CAPTAIN. You're not on the list.

ARGA. Not on the list! Must be a mistake. The General is dying to see her. And who wouldn't. Just look at that face.

JUDITH. Arga, please. *(She makes an alluring face.)*

CAPTAIN #2. Woman, what have you there? Once more, I repeat, what have you there?

JUDITH. It's a wig box. You never seen a wig box before?

CAPTAIN #2. What do you keep in there?

JUDITH. A wig.

CAPTAIN #2. Why do you bring with you a disguise? The truth, woman!

JUDITH. You force me to admit what could prove an embarrassment.

CAPTAIN. The truth or your lives shall pay the forfeit.

ARGA. You'd better tell him.

JUDITH. I was rather hoping to be asked to spend the night. I can't imagine you'll have proper facilities for me to wash my hair in the morning. Thus the wig.

CAPTAIN. Open the box.

ARGA. The catch is tricky. I order these cases all the way from Caledonia.

*(ARGA opens it and it's empty.)*

CAPTAIN. It's empty.

JUDITH. *(to ARGA)* Well, ain't that swell. You remembered the box but forgot to put in the wig.

ARGA. I can't remember everything.

CAPTAIN. I shall speak to my superior officer. You women will remain here.

*(The two* CAPTAINS *exit.)*

ARGA. What's your plan if by some miracle the General does receive you?

JUDITH. Somehow I've got to get him alone and somehow I've gotta get a hold of his sword.

ARGA. That's a lot of "gettin'."

JUDITH. The only way I'm gonna relieve the General of his sword is using this face and this figure.

ARGA. I'm not leaving you here by yourself.

JUDITH. Arga, we've gone over this.

ARGA. I'm not budging.

JUDITH. Well, hide yourself behind that pouf. And don't do a thing unless I give you a signal.

ARGA. What's the signal?

JUDITH. Hmmmm. I'll um – I'll touch my right – um - ear. Oh, and give me Nathan's calming potion.

*(*ARGA *gives her the tiny vial.)*

ARGA. For your nerves?

JUDITH. To keep the Assyrian lion from roaring. *(She pours the vial into the large wine carafe on the table.)* Now make yourself scarce. I hear the beast approaching. I need to organize my torso.

*(*JUDITH *tucks the vials into her cleavage.* ARGA *hides behind the pouf.* HOLOFERNES *enters with two* CAPTAINS *and* URDAMANI*.)*

HOLOFERNES. The Widow Manasses, I would sooner have expected a visit from a unicorn.

JUDITH. I suppose there's a compliment hidden in there somewhere.

CAPTAIN. General, the Widow was accompanied by her handmaiden.

HOLOFERNES. I see no handmaiden.

JUDITH. She left. She's a sensitive girl. She got the impression she wasn't wanted.

HOLOFERNES. You are here then alone and unprotected?

**JUDITH.** I must rely on your good intentions.

**HOLOFERNES.** A woman's presence enlivens these harsh surroundings.

**URDAMANI.** General, do not trust this citizeness of Bethulia. She could well be armed.

**HOLOFERNES.** *(aroused)* Are you armed?

**JUDITH.** I assure you I have absolutely nothing underneath this gown.

**HOLOFERNES.** I'd say there's plenty under that gown and just as dangerous.

**URDAMANI.** General, if you long for feminine company, we have slave women quarantined at the edge of camp. Indeed, the women of Nin are prepared to perform for you their Dance of the Fishers.

**HOLOFERNES.** I have no interest in the lumpish, hairy arm pitted, horse faced women of Nin. Not when there is enchantment in this very tent. Leave us, Eunuch.

*(**HOLOFERNES** stretches out provocatively on the pouf.)*

**URDAMANI.** But General —

**HOLOFERNES.** Leave us!

**URDAMANI.** As you wish, your Excellency. I shall remain with your men just outside.

*(The jealous eunuch sticks his tongue out at **JUDITH**, plays with his titties to show his disrespect and exits with the two **CAPTAINS**.)*

**HOLOFERNES.** Do forgive the devotion of my Chief Eunuch.

**JUDITH.** For a moment I thought he was going to bitch slap me.

*(**HOLOFERNES** rises and pours himself some wine.)*

**HOLOFERNES.** Some wine, my lady? It is the finest in the region.

**JUDITH.** Confiscated, no doubt.

**HOLOFERNES.** But of course. It gives the grapes a uniquely dark acidity. I insist that you join me in a flagon.

**JUDITH.** Prudence dictates.

*(He drinks from both goblets.)*

**JUDITH**. A man who likes his liquor. Drink away.

**HOLOFERNES**. Drunk or sober, I cannot imagine you being less than clever.

**JUDITH**. I thought most men despise a clever woman.

**HOLOFERNES**. I am not most men. And by your pluck in passing through the Eastern gate, I'd say you are definitely a most singular example of your sex. *(intrigued)* Why do you come here? The truth.

**JUDITH**. Why do you think?

**HOLOFERNES**. To kill me.

**JUDITH**. Why should I kill someone whose victory would mean a mortal defeat for my enemies?

**HOLOFERNES**. Your enemies?

**JUDITH**. Surely, you have heard the outrageous calumnies surrounding my name? I am reviled by my own people as a vulgar bathhouse girl from the left bank of the River Jordan; an adventuress who married an old man for his fortune and squandered a mountain of gold on gowns, jewels and pleasure.

**HOLOFERNES**. Yes, those tales have reached even this military outpost.

**JUDITH**. I've done my level best to be a respectable matriarch. A credit to the community. But all my fine efforts have been met with dismissal and ridicule. So I say, "fuck 'em."

**HOLOFERNES**. And you are willing to ally yourself with the Assyrian conquest of Judea?

**JUDITH**. Well, surveying the pros and cons of the situation, your side appears to be the clear winner. And I do so admire a winner.

**HOLOFERNES**. The Assyrians. I hold them in greater contempt than I do your people. As long as I live, the Assyrians will cower and crawl like slugs in the mud. They'd rather remain compliant mules, blind to the bloodlust around them, than rebel and be singled out for the lash. *(brooding darkly)* They deserve me. I am a tomb without a corpse, an empty grave.

**JUDITH**. You're certainly in a mood.

**HOLOFERNES**. I can forgo my introspection. Your feminine essence makes me feverish with longing.

**JUDITH**. Oh, we're back to my essence again, are we?

**HOLOFERNES**. Yes, we will always return to that. *(suddenly alarmed)* Something is not quite right. I cannot help but feel the presence of leering eyes upon us.

*(**ARGA** fears that she's been discovered behind the pouf.)*

**JUDITH**. Except for the occasional mosquito, we're quite alone in this tent.

**HOLOFERNES**. My Eunuch no doubt has his ears pressed against the canvas. *(with urgency)* Come with me to my fortress in Nineveh. Tonight. I'll have my men saddle the camels.

**JUDITH**. I'd much rather stay here. I've never been inside a military camp before. I find its masculine ambience highly stimulating.

**HOLOFERNES**. But in Nineveh I can provide you with a dozen handmaidens to do your every bidding.

**JUDITH**. Tonight, General, allow me to be *your* handmaiden.

**HOLOFERNES**. I see your eyes have settled on my long curved scimitar.

**JUDITH**. Is that what you call it?

**HOLOFERNES**. The sharpest blade in all Assyria. With one strike, I can cut off a man's head.

**JUDITH**. Just think what you could do with a brisket.

*(He puts his arms around her and they sway gently to the subtle rhythms of the music coming from outside.)*

**HOLOFERNES**. The women of Nin are practicing their dance. Hear the beat of the drum.

**JUDITH**. Mmmm. General, you put your heart and soul into your dancing. You're breaking into a sweat.

**HOLOFERNES**. Do you find that distasteful?

**JUDITH.** I like a man who gets worked up. You should make yourself comfortable. After all, it is your tent.

*(She reclines on the pouf.)*

**HOLOFERNES.** How should you like me to make myself comfortable?

**JUDITH.** You can remove your shift for a start.

**HOLOFERNES.** Easily accomplished.

*(He begins to remove his shift.)*

**JUDITH.** Slowly. In time to the music. Yeah, you got it.

**HOLOFERNES.** I should not let my scimitar out of sight.

**JUDITH.** I won't play with it, unless you ask me.

*(He removes his sword and belt. And pulls off his shift. He's wearing a smaller shift underneath.)*

**JUDITH.** You dropped something.

*(He turns around and bends over and then sees what she's up to. Amused and titillated, he chuckles and wags his finger as if saying " Naughty girl.")*

I've always been fascinated by the view from backstage.

**HOLOFERNES.** If you wish, I could have my Chief Eunuch shave my anal crack.

**JUDITH.** I wouldn't want you to go to any trouble.

**HOLOFERNES.** It would give him the greatest pleasure. Indeed, it would justify his very existence.

**JUDITH.** Well, let's hold off on that for a bit.

**HOLOFERNES.** You maddening creature. You engorge me with lustful fantasy. *(He joins her on the pouf.)*

**JUDITH.** That's the general idea.

**HOLOFERNES.** You are a born seductress.

**JUDITH.** I've always had a way with the boys.

**HOLOFERNES.** I should like to know more. *(His eyelids become heavy. He stifles a yawn. The drug is beginning to take effect.)*

**JUDITH.** You with me?

**HOLOFERNES.** Oh yes. Continue. *(He reclines on the pouf.)*

**JUDITH.** Well um…the first fellow who gave me the fish eye was named Absalom. He was an older man and quite sophisticated. I've always had a yen for sophisticated men.

**HOLOFERNES.** I'm sophisticated.

**JUDITH.** We'll see about that. This gentleman was an inventor. He came up with a contraption to tell the time of day. Called it a clock. Never caught on.

(**HOLOFERNES** *momentarily closes his eyes.* **ARGA***'s head pops up from behind the pouf. She catches* **JUDITH***'s eye and gives her the thumbs up. She ducks down again.* **JUDITH** *continues to mesmerize* **HOLOFERNES** *into slumber.*)

After Absalom, there was Josiah. Jeremiah. Jedediah, Hezekiah. Abraham, Martin and John. Omar, Levi. Reuben.

(**HOLOFERNES** *appears quite asleep. In fact, he's snoring.*)

My Lord? My Lord? Out cold and laid out like a mackerel.

(*She pulls his sword out of the scabbard. She holds it aloft and moves closer to the supine* **HOLOFERNES**, *prepared to chop off his head. He suddenly stirs.* )

**HOLOFERNES.** *(slurring)* Who was the last one?

**JUDITH.** Reuben. Maybe we should take a break. Your eyelids are shutting tighter than the back door to a pyramid.

**HOLOFERNES.** I don't know what's come over me. Perhaps it is the bouquet of your rose scented tresses and your breath…

**JUDITH.** My breath?

**HOLOFERNES.** Your sweet breath which evokes a far off grove of cinnamon.

**JUDITH.** Oh.

**HOLOFERNES**. All conspire to drowse me. You of the dove's eyes and the proud swan's throat, I must take leave of you for a brief moment. Yes, I must take my leave.

**JUDITH**. Must you?

*(He stumbles out of the tent, leaving his sword held by* **JUDITH**. *But instantly returns for it. He exits again.* **ARGA** *leaves her hiding place.* **JUDITH** *is in a vortex of emotion.)*

**ARGA**. You're doing great.

**JUDITH**. No, I'm not. Arga, this man – this minotaur has unlocked within me a perverse but undeniable passion. Only the barest resolve keeps me from utter submission.

**ARGA**. Mistress, what are you saying?

**JUDITH**. You know what I'm saying. I'm in over my head. Contrary to popular belief, I haven't felt the touch of a man's hands since the death of Manasses and trust me, *that* wasn't exactly party time in old Babylon.

**ARGA**. You must think of your people.

**JUDITH**. I can no longer see the faces of my people, only his face. His body. Why, why, why, why am I condemned to this diabolical longing?

**ARGA**. You're attracted to danger. It's very common. Years ago, I met a man who brought out in me a similar recklessness. His name was Pincus. Can't even talk about it. I broke out in a rash.

**JUDITH**. How do I free myself from this hunger?

**ARGA**. *(with a new intense fervor)* Think not of the fire in your loins, but of the fires that fan the walls of the poor people of Bethulia. Think not of your hunger for his flesh but of the famished women whose breasts no longer can feed their starving babies. Think not of your moans of desire but of the moaning of the murdered children of Judea!

*(***JUDITH*** *falls to her knees in prayer.* **ARGA** *joins her and holds her in her arms.)*

**JUDITH**. Dear Lord, look down on me, a feeble thing unless thou sendeth strength!

(**HOLOFERNES** *returns, recharged, with a large erection tenting his tunic, and carrying his sword.*)

**HOLOFERNES**. Who is this? Ah, yes, your handmaiden. I thought you had departed.

**ARGA**. *(desperately fumbling)* I'm a creature of whim. Mercurial.

**JUDITH**. My Lord, I thought you were drowsy.

**HOLOFERNES**. I was feeling indisposed but helped myself to a cunning brew of Ahswaganda root, Avena Sativa, Saw Palmetto and jalapeno peppers. Its restorative powers are miraculous.

*(He grinds his hips lasciviously.)*

**JUDITH**. Evidently. Arga, the General and I have much to discuss. Wait for me without.

**HOLOFERNES**. No. It has been far too long since I've enjoyed the pleasure of a woman. Like a starving man at a banquet, I must deny myself nothing. I shall feast on the two of you. Yes. Two fine succulent birds.

**ARGA**. Oh, I'm just an old stewing hen.

**JUDITH**. Yeah. You don't want her. I've seen her take a sponge bath. Her knockers practically touch the parquet.

**HOLOFERNES**. Silence! I will not be denied my revelry! I shall take the handmaiden first, while you watch her humiliation. Wouldst that not amuse you?

**JUDITH**. I'd prefer a comic.

*(He pushes **ARGA** over the pouf, her face towards the audience. He goes behind her and throws her gown up, exposing her hind quarters to him.)*

**HOLOFERNES**. Ahhh. I am fortune's most blessed. This stern hag hath the firm, proud buttocks of a youthful bawd.

**ARGA**. *(mortified)* Don't let appearances fool you.

**JUDITH.** *(desperate to save* **ARGA**) Your highness, take me first. *(Shimmying)* I'll get things going.

**HOLOFERNES.** Woman, I give the orders! But as a General well versed in military maneuvers, I must strategize; which port of entry do I attack first?

**JUDITH.** Either way looks like a trap.

*(With the general distracted,* **JUDITH** *grabs the sword.)*

**HOLOFERNES.** *(he mounts* **ARGA**) I shall begin with the ateway least trafficked. Victory!

**ARGA.** Ahhhhhhhhgh!

*(***JUDITH** *raises the sword in triumph.)*

**JUDITH.** For the Jews!

*(blackout)*

## SCENE TEN

*(Lights up and* **JUDITH** *is holding his severed head.)*

**JUDITH.** The deed is done. The Bull of Asshur is now but a skull draped in cold flesh, blind eyes staring, ears that hear nothing, lips that kiss no more. Arga, how's your ass?

**ARGA.** I would be amiss if I said I wasn't in severe discomfort.

**JUDITH.** We mustn't tarry. Let us place the Generals' head in the wig box and beat it.

*(***ARGA*** *moves in front of* **JUDITH**, *blocking the view of the General's head.)*

**JUDITH.** Can you fit it in there?

**ARGA.** We've had some big hairdos in that box, complete with switches, braids and wiglets. He'll fit.

*(***ARGA*** *finishes and closes the lid of the wig box.)*

**JUDITH.** Then we have completed our grim task.

*(***NAOMI***, still bound and gagged, hobbles in. She sees the two ladies and grunts.)*

**JUDITH.** Naomi! This cannot be!

**ARGA.** She's alive!

**JUDITH.** You're alive! You're alive!

*(***JUDITH*** *pulls the gag out of her mouth and begins untying her.)*

**NAOMI.** The General was keeping me on the other side of this curtain. I heard everything.

**JUDITH.** *(embracing her)* My darling, how we have mourned you.

**NAOMI.** Wow. You took his head.

**JUDITH.** It's in the wig box.

**ARGA.** This is no time to go down memory lane. We've gotta run!

*(The two* **CAPTAINS** *enter the tent, looking for Holofernes.)*

**CAPTAIN**. General! General!

*(The three women are stunned.)*

What goes on here? *(He sees the dead body of Holofernes.)* You killed him. You killed Holofernes.

**CAPTAIN #2**. The General has been murdered!

**JUDITH**. I, Judith of Bethulia, am his executioner.

**CAPTAIN**. You killed the General. *(He looks offstage to perhaps his entire legion.)* All hail Judith! General Holofernes is dead!

**CAPTAINS / OFF STAGE ARMY**. All hail Judith! General Holofernes is dead!

**ARGA**. You do not condemn her for this act?

**CAPTAIN #2**. Holofernes was a cruel and vicious despot who commanded his army through terror.

*(The first **CAPTAIN** opens the wig box.)*

**CAPTAIN**. So this is from which his deadly power stemmed.

**JUDITH**. The head. May we have it?

**CAPTAIN**. Oy gevalte. Please, by all means, take it with you.

**NAOMI**. Wait a minute. Are you – the Jew? Ruby's friend?

**CAPTAIN**. Yes. I have kept my faith a dark secret. But no more. Here they call me Lamech. Henceforth, I shall return to my birth name. David Littman.

**ARGA**. It's a good name.

**CAPTAIN**. The eunuch could return at any moment. We must get you ladies out of the camp.

**JUDITH**. The sooner the better.

**CAPTAIN**. Quick! The black night shall swallow thee. Let us be gone!

*(They run out.)*

## END OF SCENE

## SCENE ELEVEN

*(Judith's home. Days later.* **NATHAN** *enters with his arm around* **NAOMI** *'s slim waist. They are followed on by Simon and* **OZIAS**. *All are joyful.)*

**OZIAS**. Let the triumphant breath of trumpets blow the news to the four winds. Judea is saved!

**SIMON**. My friend, you have been exclaiming those same words for the last five days!

**OZIAS**. And I shall shout them till the end of time! Without their leader, Holofernes, the Assyrian army flailed, panicked and fled. Listen, from this high promontory one can hear the thousands celebrating our victory in the village square.

*(The roar of the crowd can be briefly heard in the distance.)*

**NATHAN**. I must give voice to my own private ejaculation. My beautiful Naomi is alive.

**NAOMI**. Safe within these walls. The hallowed fortress of my Mistress Judith.

**NATHAN**. Safe in my eternal devotion. My Naomi, do allow the curtain of fear to lift from your troubled brow.

**NAOMI**. It's hard.

**NATHAN**. My undying wish is to see you bromidic and bright as a moon happy night pouring light on the dew.

**NAOMI**. Has the storm of war truly passed over us?

**NATHAN**. Beyond that window lies a golden sun and the sweet silver song of a lark.

**SIMON**. Walk on, Naomi, with hope in your heart.

**OZIAS**. Walk on towards the sacred chuppah.

**NATHAN**. Under that ennobled canopy we shall soon be joined in holy marriage.

**NAOMI**. No longer Naomi Lynn Barbara Renee Beckerman, but Naomi, wife of Nathan.

SIMON. On that wondrous day, we shall bedeck the sanctuary with the most extravagant of flowers.

NATHAN. By the grace of Judith's hand, the temple of worship still stands.

OZIAS. And yet, this house of Manasses, which should by all measure, be a place of triumphant joy, has the air of mournful retreat.

NAOMI. My mistress does not regard her act as one of triumph.

SIMON. I hear that she begged the Patriarchs to remove the head of Holofernes from the lance on which it is set above the Eastern Gate.

OZIAS. I wonder now that the peril is past if in her thoughts there is not some vague nameless sense of dread of her own self that could do such a deed. Ah, the lady comes.

(JUDITH *enters in white. Lilies crown her head.*)

NAOMI. Mistress, it's been days since you've left your shadow draped boudoir.

JUDITH. It does my heart good to see my fair Naomi cradled in her beloved's arms.

SIMON. Great lady, I thought you would be clad in cloth of gold, not in the white robes of a Priestess.

OZIAS. Like some victorious Chief returned from war, she lays aside her armor.

JUDITH. Look not to me as a General, young Ozias. God was the hand. I was but the sword. Yes, the sword was I, and he, the hand that smote.

NATHAN. But you have taught us that it is in *our* mortal hands to create our destinies, that God's greatest gift to us is our free will.

JUDITH. Well, if I said it I meant it.

NAOMI. Mistress Judith, please join with us in our celebration of the glorious victory you have wrought.

JUDITH. I cannot.

SIMON. You have the manner of one who is guilty of some unconscionable sin.

**JUDITH**. That terrible night I discovered something in myself, ugly, dark and violent. Although no one condemns my act, I condemn myself.

**NAOMI**. You mustn't. You mustn't. It's not fair.

**JUDITH**. My children, I have decided that from this day forth I shall dwell apart, alone in this house, where laughter and high spirits are not welcome. Only the sorrowful and depressed shall find the door unbarred. The more farbisseneh the face the better. I shall deny myself even the simple pleasure of looking out of this tower window, so high above the ground, with my beloved view of the open sea and sky.

**NAOMI**. Please, don't leave us. We love you so.

(**ARGA** *enters.*)

**ARGA**. Mistress, there is a leper here to see you.

**JUDITH**. A visit from a leper suits my mood. Show him in. *(to the others)* See? This is the new tone.

**ARGA**. *(to the offstage* **LEPER***)* You may enter. Just don't touch anything.

(*A linen wrapped* **LEPER** *enters, his face shrouded.*)

**LEPER**. Bless you, Widow, for granting me audience.

**JUDITH**. What can I do for you?

**LEPER**. The citizens of Bethulia are now showering you with praise, but we who dwell in the Valley of Death, have long known of your courage and grace. I have but one valued possession. The last remnant of my former life of luxury. May I give it to you?

(**ARGA** *mimes behind the* **LEPER***'s back, "Don't touch it!")*

**JUDITH**. If it is indeed as valuable as you say, exchange it for gold or at least for soup.

**LEPER**. Giving is the last bit of humanity that we outcasts have left.

**OZIAS**. Look at his hand. It is free of sores. This be not a leper at all!

(**OZIAS** *pulls off the shroud. It is indeed* **URDAMANI**! *He brandishes a dagger.*)

URDAMANI. If I have a disease, it is a fatal illness of the spirit. You, whore of Judea, hath slain my Prince. His leonine head displayed on the Eastern Gate has been removed. Where is it? Give it to me!

JUDITH. Poor tragic soul. It exists no more.

URDAMANI. I don't believe you. You lie!

ARGA. She speaks the truth. It was tossed into the open sea.

URDAMANI. Nooooo!!!! Hebrew Witch, you have murdered my master and now deny me that cherished token of veneration. For that you shall die!!

*(He is about to attack* **JUDITH** *and then suddenly stops.)*

I cannot. I cannot go forth. Tis the poisonous spirit of Holofernes that demands retribution. I am not and never have been of his kind. I sought his love and only his love and now I shall be damned for it. Judith, I ask nothing of thee.

*(Inspirational music swells. A miracle is occurring.)*

NAOMI. Look at the Eunuch!

NATHAN. He has the countenance of one possessed.

(**URDAMANI** *sways and then is overcome with the power of God.)*

URDAMANI. There is something powerful pulling me to earth. Heavy, weighted, and yet full of the stuff of life. O stars above! Can it be but the Lord hath given of me a fresh cornucopia of manly fruit. *(He turns to* **ARGA***)* Feel it! Tell me it is so.

(**ARGA** *gives a quick squeeze to his crotch.)*

ARGA. *(with slight distaste)* Tis so.

(**SIMON** *and* **OZIAS** *fall to their knees in rapture.)*

SIMON. God has once more made himself known.

OZIAS. Sing his praises.

NATHAN. Thank thee, God of the Israelites.

NAOMI. Thank thee, Lord.

JUDITH. I'm sincerely very happy for you.

**URDAMANI.** I have found a twisted pathway to the ancient faith of the Jews.

**ARGA.** If you are indeed embracing the Jewish lifestyle, you must prepare yourself for yet other surgery; that of circumcision.

**URDAMANI.** Remove a part of my precious new organ?

**ARGA.** You wanna be a Jew or doncha?

**URDAMANI.** *(resigned, with a shrug)* Take the foreskin. So be it.

*(A loud din is heard outside. Ugly cries of "Judith must die!" "Death to the Jews!" "Revenge!")*

**NAOMI.** Those ugly cries from just outside. What could be happening?

**URDAMANI.** *(with urgency)* I was not alone. I was accompanied by a renegade legion of the Assyrian soldiers. They seek reprisal for the death of their leader.

**NATHAN.** What sort of reprisal?

**URDAMANI.** Their mission is to set fire to the temple and to this very abode.

**SIMON.** We must remove the women at once to safety.

**NATHAN.** Do not fear, we shall stop them!

**OZIAS.** It will be their blood spilt on the temple steps!

**JUDITH.** No! Not one more drop of blood must be shed. As long as the murderer of Holofernes lives there shall be reprisals.

**NAOMI.** Mistress Judith, what are you saying?

**ARGA.** She's getting one of her ideas. I don't like it.

*(Two hooded Assyrian **GUARDS** burst into the room, brandishing large sabers. **ARGA** and **NAOMI** scream in terror. )*

**GUARD #1.** We have come for the women. All must die!! Holofernes will be avenged!!

*(**JUDITH** throws herself in front of the cowering, terrified **ARGA** and **NAOMI**. **NATHAN**, Simon and **OZIAS** step forward, but are helplessly unarmed. )*

**JUDITH**. Jackals, away from us, you hear!!!

*(The two* **GUARDS** *advance menacingly. )*

**GUARD #2**. She must be slain with the sword of Holofernes!

**JUDITH**. Yes, dear Nathan, it is in our hands to create our own destinies. It is in our hands.

*(She runs to the open window.)*

**ARGA**. *(sobbing)* Mistress Judith!

**GUARD #2**. She must not jump!

**NATHAN**. She cannot be stopped.

**JUDITH**. Judea is saved!

> **(JUDITH** *leaps from the window. Thunderous music swells to a grand inspirational operatic climax.)*

## THE END